we love you, Rosie!

written by
Cynthia Rylant

illustrated by
Linda Davick

Beach Lane Books · New York London Toronto Sydney New Delhi

Rosie Day and Night

Hello, Rosie.

Did you just wake up?

Do you love the DAY?

Look at Rosie run!

Look at Rosie play!

Rosie runs and plays
and runs and plays
ALL DAY!

Hello, Rosie.

Are you tired?

Do you love the NIGHT?

Look at Rosie sleep.

Look at Rosie dream.

Rosie sleeps and dreams
and sleeps and dreams
ALL NIGHT.

Good night, Rosie.
We love you.

Rosie Good and Bad

Hello, Rosie.

Are you being GOOD?

GOOD sitting, Rosie!

GOOD barking, Rosie!

GOOD eating, Rosie!

Rosie is very GOOD.

Hello, Rosie.
Are you being BAD?

Oops. BAD eating, Rosie!

Rosie,
you are sometimes GOOD
and you are sometimes BAD.

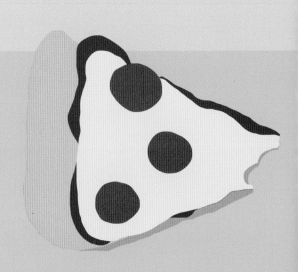

But you are always Rosie!
And we love you.

Rosie In and Out

Hello, Rosie.

Do you want IN?

Rosie wants IN the house.

Rosie wants IN the kitchen.

Rosie
wants
IN
IN
IN.

Hello, Rosie.

Do you want OUT?

Rosie wants OUT of the kitchen.

Rosie wants OUT of the house.

Rosie wants OUT OUT OUT.

and Rosie OUT.

And, Rosie, we love you.

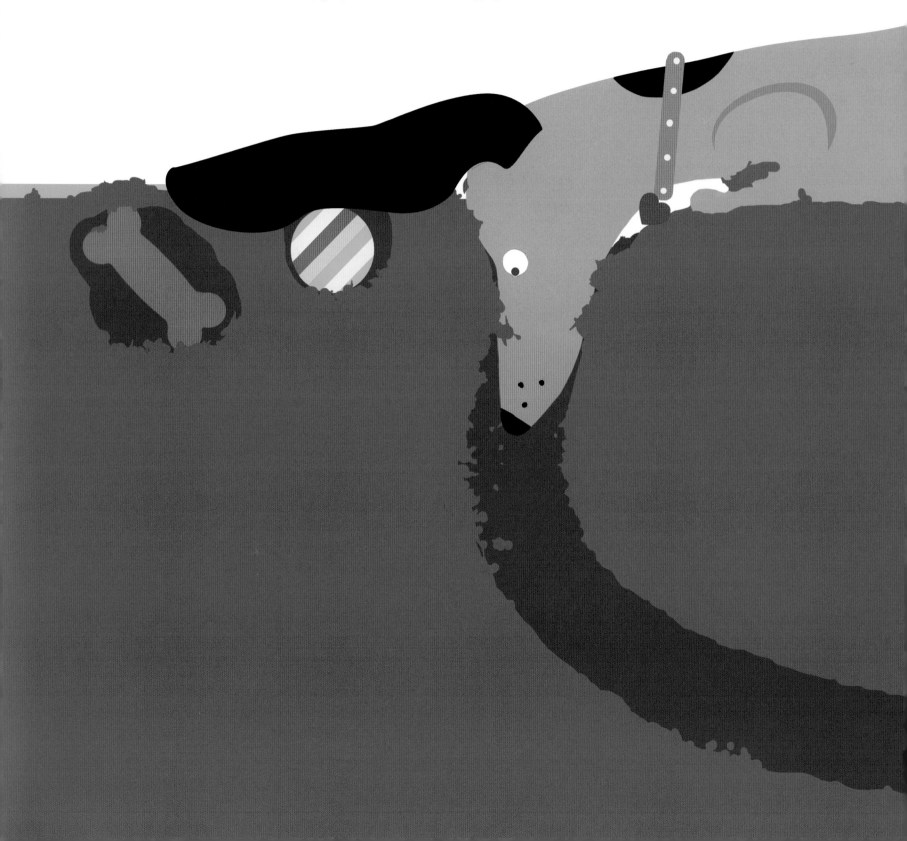

Rosie Lost and Found

Hello, Rosie.
What have you LOST?
Have you LOST a ball?
Have you LOST a bone?
Have you LOST a friend?
What has Rosie LOST?

Hello, Rosie.

What have you FOUND?

Have you FOUND a ball?

Have you FOUND a bone?

Have you FOUND a friend?

Rosie, you have LOST
and you have FOUND!

And we love you!

Rosie Up and Down

Hello, Rosie.

Do you want to come UP?

Okay. UP go the front feet!

UP go the back feet!

UP goes the tail!

Rosie is going UP!

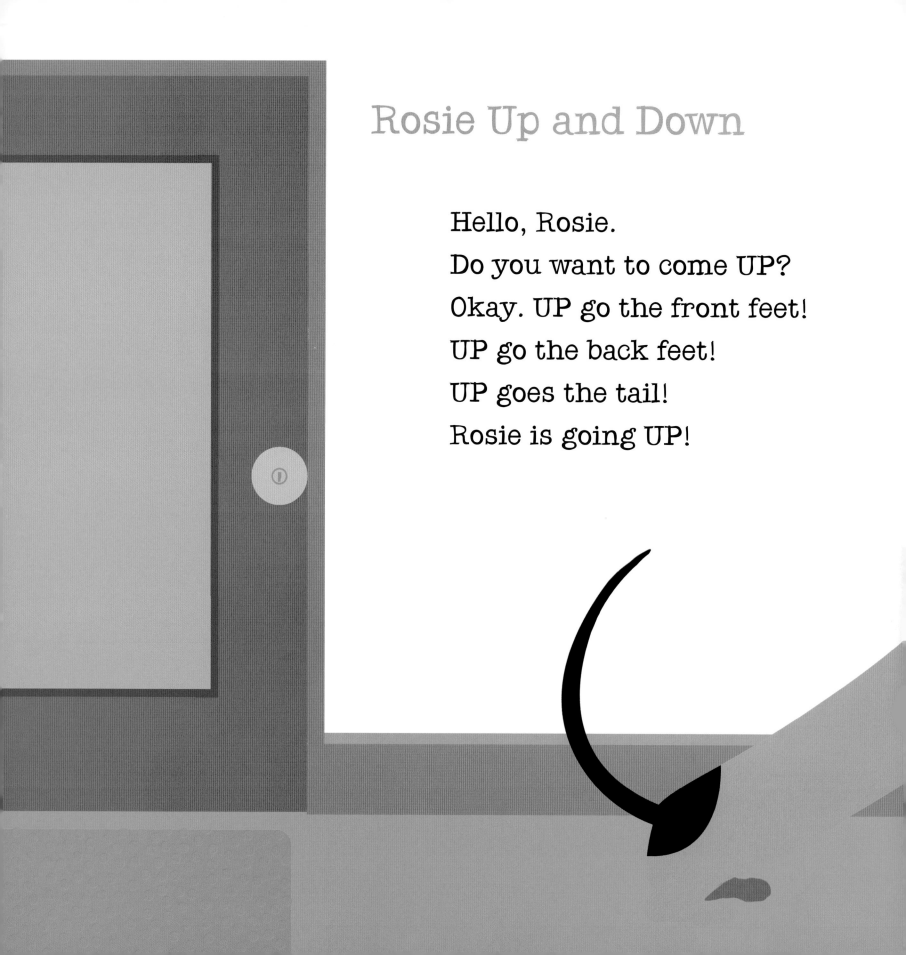

Hello, Rosie.

Do you want to go DOWN?

Okay. DOWN go the front feet!

DOWN go the back feet!

DOWN goes the tail!

Rosie is going DOWN!

But Rosie likes UP better.

UP is better.

UP is much better!

Rosie, you are UP.

And we love you.

Rosie Here and There

Hello, Rosie.

Do you want to stay HERE?

HERE you have a blanket.

HERE you have a bed.

HERE you have a nice octopus.

Hello, Rosie.

Do you want to go THERE?

THERE you have lightning.

THERE you have thunder.

THERE you have a wet giraffe.

HERE, Rosie?

Or THERE, Rosie?

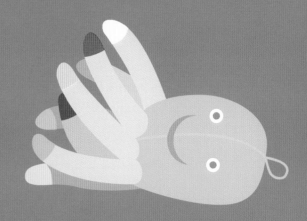

Yes, Rosie, HERE.

Where we love you!

For Anna
–C. R.

For the Cricket
–L. D.

BEACH LANE BOOKS

An imprint of Simon & Schuster Children's Publishing Division
1230 Avenue of the Americas, New York, New York 10020
Text copyright © 2017 by Cynthia Rylant
Illustrations copyright © 2017 by Linda Davick
All rights reserved, including the right of reproduction in whole or in part in any form.
BEACH LANE BOOKS is a trademark of Simon & Schuster, Inc.
For information about special discounts for bulk purchases, please contact Simon & Schuster Special Sales
at 1-866-506-1949 or business@simonandschuster.com.
The Simon & Schuster Speakers Bureau can bring authors to your live event.
For more information or to book an event, contact the Simon & Schuster Speakers Bureau at 1-866-248-3049
or visit our website at www.simonspeakers.com.
Book design by Lauren Rille.
The text for this book was set in Quattro Tempi.
Manufactured in China
1216 SCP
First Edition
10 9 8 7 6 5 4 3 2 1
Library of Congress Cataloging-in-Publication Data
Names: Rylant, Cynthia, author.
Title: We love you, Rosie! / Cynthia Rylant ; illustrated by Linda Davick.
Description: First edition. | New York : Beach Lane Books, [2016] | Summary: "Rosie is a family dog
who goes about her day exploring opposites. No matter what she does, her family always loves her"– Provided by publisher.
Identifiers: LCCN 2015029888| ISBN 9781442465114 (hardback) | ISBN 9781442465121 (e-book)
Subjects: | CYAC: Dogs–Fiction. | English language–Synonyms and antonyms–Fiction. | Family life–Fiction. | BISAC: JUVENILE
FICTION / Animals / Dogs. | JUVENILE FICTION / Concepts / Opposites. | JUVENILE FICTION / Family / General
(see also headings under Social Issues).
Classification: LCC PZ7.R982 Wc 2016 | DDC [E]–dc23 LC record available at http://lccn.loc.gov/2015029888